Table of Contents

Las Vegas Revealed:1931-1932

A Time Traveler's Handbook

By Derrick Fitzgerald

Welcome to the Retrorsum Time Travel Book Series
Las Vegas Revealed: 1931–1932
A Time Traveler's Handbook

So you've arrived—or are preparing to arrive—in Las Vegas during one of its most transformative periods. Whether you're simply an armchair adventurer or a curious traveler who's actually managed to cross the temporal boundaries, what follows is a practical, immersive guide to surviving and even thriving in 1931–1932 Nevada.

This handbook is not a technical manual on the mechanics of time travel. Instead, it is a curated resource designed to help you navigate the early 1930s with know-how and confidence. Inside, you'll find real information about accommodations, food, social customs, dangers, and opportunities—much of it drawn directly from historical records, such as *The Las Vegas Age* (one of Vegas's earliest newspapers), as well as accounts from others who manage to traverse the boundaries of time and space to a far earlier version of modern-day Las Vegas.

Las Vegas in 1931 is a city in transition. The Great Depression is just beginning, the Boulder Dam project is drawing thousands of laborers, and Prohibition is fueling both hardship and opportunity. Legalized gambling has just been approved, and this dusty little town is on the verge of becoming one of the leading entertainment spots—not only in the U.S., but eventually the world.

Should you find yourself walking the streets of 1930s Las Vegas, uncertain whether that small den or gin mill is safe or a trap waiting to spring—this guide just might spare you a great deal of trouble or a night in jail.

Why 1931–1932? A City at the Edge

Las Vegas in 1931 isn't really a vacation spot—it is a ragtag boomtown teetering between collapse and transformation. With the Great Depression tightening its grip and construction of the Boulder Dam now underway, thousands of job seekers are pouring into the city in search of work and survival.

The sudden population surge is pushing local infrastructure beyond its limits. The few hotels that currently exist are filled to capacity, and makeshift tent cities are beginning to spring up along the town's outskirts, offering little protection from the unforgiving desert climate. Anyone arriving during this time is quickly confronted with the realities of life in a city bursting at the seams—overcrowding, limited access to basic supplies, and a growing scene of desperation and petty crime.

Both longtime residents and newly arrived workers are facing hardship and instability. Yet, from this chaos there is this spirit of grit and resilience—the early foundation of a city determined to reinvent itself.

One of the most infamous districts you'll encounter is Block 16, located on North First Street between Ogden and Stewart Avenues. Established in 1905, this red-light district **was** the only place in town where liquor could be legally served outside of hotels. During Prohibition, hooch **was** ubiquitous and easily found in the various gin mills or speakeasies.

By 1931, Block 16 has evolved into a magnet for saloons, gambling dens, and underground speakeasies like The Arizona Club (one of the first saloons in Vegas), the Pastime, the Green Lantern, and many others. It is also known for its flourishing trade in prostitution and bootlegging—activities that are often tolerated by authorities in exchange for bribes or political favors. One particularly distinctive joint is called the Desert Inn Nightclub, a Black-owned venue featuring Southern jazz and homestyle Southern cooking. In the book *Retrorsum*, Will spoke fondly of this place, as it is relatively free from the harsh segregation rules of 1930s Las Vegas.

Law enforcement raids do occur, but they rarely have any lasting impact. Speakeasies can be shut down one night and reopen the next, their patrons undeterred by the occasional raid. As Will's original journal notes on many occasions, the rhythm of vice in Block 16 is relentless—raids are seen more as inconveniences than deterrents. Bartenders often have hidden compartments ready, lookouts are usually stationed near doors, and regulars know how to vanish when the signal is given.

Despite the risk, the district thrives, fueled by a shared understanding between patrons, proprietors, and even certain officials: people need an escape, and Block 16 is more than willing to provide it. For time travelers, it remains a vivid glimpse into a city unafraid to bend the rules—one drink, one deal, one whispered password at a time.

<u>Traveler's tip:</u> Blend in! Speak politely and don't draw unnecessary attention—especially with unfamiliar clothing, language, or behavior. Carry only as much cash as you think you'll need; flashing too much will get you noticed for all the wrong reasons. Also stay mindful of potential raids, heed local advice and warnings. For time travelers, raids are an inherent risk of exposure and must be taken seriously.

The Gamble That Changed Everything

On March 19, 1931, Nevada legalized gambling in a desperate bid to revive its economy amid the Great Depression. Alongside the massive Boulder Dam project, this move sparked a wave of change. Just two weeks later, Clark County began issuing gaming licenses—officially launching Las Vegas's transformation into the gambling capital of the world.

The very first license was granted to Mayme Stocker and JH Morgan, owners of the Northern Club on Fremont Street. A shrewd businesswoman, Stocker operates a modest but well-known establishment that offers patrons a legal place to play cards and dice games along with whiskey. Her name may not appear on any neon signs of today, but her role in Las Vegas history is pivotal.

It isn't glamorous yet—no neon lights, no resort-like amenities or such. Most venues are modest, consisting of a few slot machines and card tables, where locals and travelers wager in smoke-filled rooms. The Meadows, on the east end of Fremont Street, is an exception—the first true resort in Las Vegas. Still, these backroom games and early licenses are the first small signs of what the city will one day become.

The city's transformation has begun. For anyone arriving during these formative years, it is clear that something big is taking shape—the dam project, legalized gambling, and even liberal divorce laws.

Las Vegas Unveiled: 1931–1932 — Preparation

As noted earlier, this guide does not concern itself with the mechanics of time travel—how it works, where it leads, or the technology behind it. That's someone else's specialty. Our mission here is simple: to help you navigate, survive, and thrive in 1930s Las Vegas—should you actually find yourself there.

This handbook is crafted for the hypothetical time traveler—someone bold or lucky enough to land in the heart of **Prohibition-era Las Vegas**, just as the city was beginning to transform. You'll find practical insight into the legal, social, and cultural norms of the time, including where to sleep, what to eat, how to dress, and yes, where to find a hidden speakeasy if that's your thing.

Whether you're visiting for research, adventure, or escape, this guide will help you blend in, stay safe, and make the most of your experience in a city on the edge of its own destiny.

A Time Traveler's Guide to Etiquette in Early 1930s America

Welcome, temporal explorers! As you prepare to immerse yourself in the bustling, sometimes unpredictable world of early 1930s America, understanding the social norms and expectations of the time is crucial. This guide provides an overview of etiquette in various settings, ensuring you blend seamlessly into society and avoid raising eyebrows with 21st-century habits. From dining decorum to conversational etiquette, these pointers will help you navigate the social landscape of the past with ease and grace.

When visiting Las Vegas, remember that it's a small desert town in this era, still developing its identity amid the boisterous mix of hooch, gambling, and the influx of workers from the Boulder Dam project.

Certain social formalities may be more relaxed here compared to larger cities, reflecting the town's rugged and free-spirited environment. However, maintaining a respectful demeanor and following general rules of politeness will still serve you well, even in this unique frontier of entertainment and indulgence.

The following is a list of pointers and tips that may or may not apply to you in your travels in the 4th dimension!

Dining Etiquette: A Matter of Refinement

Meals in the 1930s were more formal occasions compared to modern times, and table manners were seen as a reflection of one's character.

1. **At the Table**:

○ Wait until your host or hostess invites you to sit. If you're a gentleman, pull out the chair for your female dining companion before taking your seat. (Will encountered issues in book one of *Retrorsum* at the **Meadows**)

○ Place your napkin neatly on your lap, folded in half. Never tuck it into your shirt.

○ Bread should be broken into small pieces before eating; never bite directly into a roll.

○ Cutting a salad with a knife is now permissible under "modern etiquette," but do so sparingly.

2. **Hot Dogs and Casual Foods**: Even with casual fare like hot dogs, good manners are essential. Eat slowly, taking small bites, and chew with your mouth closed. Avoid overloading your hot dog with toppings that might spill.

Conversational Etiquette: The Art of Good Upbringing

Polite conversation in the 1930s required a mix of common sense, restraint, and attentiveness to others.

1. **Introductions**:

○ Never introduce two people unless you're sure they'll appreciate the introduction.

○ A man should wait for a woman to offer her hand during introductions; it's her privilege to decide.

2. **Polite Speech**:

○ Replace informal phrases like "Hey, what's up" with "I am delighted to know you."

○ Avoid dominating the conversation with tales about yourself. Doing so is considered ill-bred and may make you unpopular. Furthermore, it complicates your narrative about where and when you are from, potentially leading to inconsistencies.

3. **Ending a Visit**:

○ If a guest overstays their welcome, subtle hints such as lapses in conversation or a discreet yawn are acceptable ways to signal it's time to leave.

Social Etiquette in Public Spaces

Life in the 1930s followed well-defined rules of behavior, especially in public. Whether you're riding a streetcar, attending a dance, or sitting in a café, knowing the customs of the time will help you blend in—and avoid unwanted attention.

Public Transportation

A courteous individual avoids loud or disruptive behavior while riding trains, buses, or streetcars. Brief, necessary conversations are preferred, and it's considered polite to offer your seat to a lady or an elderly person. Maintaining a low profile is not only good manners—it's smart time-travel strategy.

Street Conduct

Men typically walked curbside when accompanying a lady, acting as a buffer from dust, traffic, or mud. When greeting a woman or an acquaintance, it was customary for men to tip their hats as a polite gesture. Public displays of affection were minimal; decorum was everything.

Introductions

Social formality mattered. People were usually addressed by their titles—Mr., Miss, or Doctor—unless invited to do otherwise. A lady was not introduced to a gentleman without her prior consent, and handshakes were brief and not overly firm.

Dancing

At social events or dance halls, a woman would typically wait for a man to ask her to dance—especially if the dance had been promised in advance. Speakeasies were more relaxed, but even there, respectful interaction was expected. Uninvited or aggressive behavior was frowned upon.

Card & Parlor Games

Bridge was more than a game—it was a social ritual. Players were expected to avoid snapping cards, boasting, or delaying turns. Composure and sportsmanship were valued as much as skill, and a pleasant demeanor was part of the game.

Appearance and First Impressions

In 1930s America, how one presented oneself spoke volumes about character and upbringing.

1. **Greeting Etiquette:**

   ○ A man should wait for a woman to acknowledge him first when meeting in public. After the initial meeting, a cordial greeting from both parties is appropriate.

2. **For Young Men:**

   ○ A high school boy is expected to rise when any lady enters the room, showing respect for women.

Specific Situations for Travelers

As a 21st-century time traveler, there are unique considerations for blending in while respecting the norms of the era.

1. Business Etiquette for the Temporal Visitor:

● Written Correspondence:

When writing letters or notes during your stay, use plain, unbranded white or ivory stationery if available. Avoid using modern paper or pens that could draw suspicion. A simple fountain pen and conservative handwriting style will help maintain period authenticity.

● Office Interactions (if applicable):

If you find yourself in a business or administrative setting—perhaps visiting a public office or speaking with a hotel manager—remain seated unless formally introduced or addressed directly. Rise only when appropriate, such as meeting someone for the first time or when etiquette clearly calls for it.

● General Tip:

While temporal travelers are unlikely to find themselves employed in 1930s office environments, blending into polite society may occasionally require adopting professional mannerisms. Observe and mirror the tone and posture of those around you, and avoid behavior that might seem overly casual or conspicuously modern.

2. Telephone Etiquette:

○ On shared telephone lines, keep conversations brief, especially if someone else is waiting to use the line. Remember, both language and tone matter just as they would in a face-to-face interaction. Courtesy and discretion are key.

Thoughts on Appearances:

Wearing era-appropriate attire is vital if you wish to blend into the respective period. The safest bet is to arrive with at least one change of clothing for the time, and then resort to purchasing more appropriate clothing at a local clothier such as Beckley's or J.C. Penney. This move will insure that you are wearing clothing that is suitable not only for the era, but for the location as well.

In *Retrorsum: Book One*, Will Patterson emphasized the importance of dressing appropriately—an untidy appearance reflected poor character. In that era, how you dressed spoke volumes about your self-respect and discipline. Will made it a priority to buy clothing that was suitable for 1930s soon after his arrival.

Why Dressing Appropriately Was Essential:

Social Expectations:

Dressing well demonstrates adherence to societal norms, when appearance is closely tied to respectability. A well-groomed individual is more likely to be taken seriously and respected in both professional and social settings.

Economic and Cultural Influence:

The Great Depression shapes fashion by encouraging practicality and resourcefulness. Despite limited means, people make an effort to look their best. This is viewed as a symbol of resilience and dignity.

Cultural Etiquette:

Attire matches the occasion, with clear distinctions between casual, work, and formal wear. Men typically wear suits or sport coats with ties, while women favor modest dresses or tailored separates. Accessories such as hats, gloves, and polished shoes complete the look.

Blending In and Avoiding Judgment:

Failing to meet dress standards can lead to social exclusion. "Sloppy" attire is seen as a lack of discipline. To blend in, one must reflect the era's expectations for polished, tidy appearance.

One important detail beyond clothing: men are expected to be clean-shaven. Stubble, common in the 21st century, is frowned upon. For women, a well-groomed, polished appearance with makeup is equally essential—especially in formal or evening social settings.

Language & Vocabulary

As a time traveler, one of the most noticeable changes you will encounter upon your arrival is the language of the era. Many of the euphemisms, expressions, and vocabulary will differ strikingly from what you are accustomed to in the present day.

For instance, you might hear someone respond with "ab-so-lute-ly" to express strong agreement or refer to alcohol as "giggle water." To navigate this unfamiliar linguistic landscape effectively, it is beneficial to make an effort to blend in by adopting the local language patterns. Mastering the vernacular—including phrases like "attaboy" to commend someone or describing an erroneous idea as "all wet"—will not only facilitate smoother interactions but also help you avoid drawing unwanted attention as a foreign visitor. Familiarizing yourself with common phrases, idioms, and the proper usage of terminology will greatly enhance your ability to integrate seamlessly into this strange world.

Having a PDF of common expressions from the early 1930s would be a great supplement and valuable information to assist you along the way. The following is a list of 20 often-used expressions from the era:

1. **Ab-so-lute-ly**
   An emphatic way to express strong agreement or affirmation.
2. **All Wet**
   Describing an idea or person as erroneous or misguided.
3. **Attaboy**
   A term of encouragement or praise, similar to saying "well done."
4. **Baby**
   A term of endearment for a sweetheart; also denotes something of high value or respect.
5. **Baloney**
   Nonsense!

6. **Big Cheese**

   The most important or influential person; boss.

7. **Bimbo**

   A tough guy.

8. **Copacetic**

   Wonderful, fine, all right.

9. **Crush**

   An infatuation.

10. **Dame**

    A female.

11. **Dapper**

    Stylishly neat and trim in appearance.

12. **Giggle Water**

    A term for alcoholic beverages.

13. **Hooch**

    Bootleg liquor.

14. **Joint**

    An establishment, usually selling alcohol.

15. **Razz**

    To make fun of.

16. **Swell**

    Wonderful; also refers to a rich man.

17. **Take for a Ride**

    To drive off with someone in order to bump them off.

18. **What's Eating You?**

    What's wrong.

19. **You Slay Me**

    That's funny.

20. **Keen**

    Attractive or appealing.

The Case For—And Against—Bringing Technology

As depicted in the ***Retrorsum* series**, both Will Patterson and Charles Damron brought 21st-century technology with them on their respective journeys into the past. To some, introducing modern devices into the early 1930s may seem impractical or even reckless—raising questions about feasibility, ethics, and unintended temporal consequences.

Before considering what to bring, it's essential to assess how long one intends to stay. For short-term visits—weeks or a couple of months—modern technology offers limited benefit. Immersion in the period becomes more practical, even preferable, as adapting to local tools and customs avoids the complications of powering, concealing, or—in the very unfortunate event of discovery—having to explain your futuristic devices to a 1930s local.

However, for travelers like Will Patterson, who remained in the 1930s for over a year, technology became a strategic asset. Will sought balance—embracing the simplicity of the era while using select modern tools to adapt more effectively. For him, these tools weren't luxuries but aids that softened the challenges of daily life in a pre-digital world.

Still, bringing technology carries serious risks. Devices like laptops, digital players, or portable batteries may seem useful, but maintaining and concealing them in a time with limited infrastructure can be challenging. Even minor slip-ups—a glowing screen glimpsed through a window, a modern ringtone overheard—could spark suspicion, draw unwanted attention, or worse, alter history in unpredictable ways.

The choice ultimately depends on the traveler's goals, length of stay, and tolerance for risk. While modern tools can enhance comfort and efficiency, they demand careful handling. One must ask: Does the benefit of bringing the future into the past outweigh the risk of disrupting it?

Unlike Charles, Will initially approached this question with a more relaxed attitude. But over time, his outlook changed. As his understanding of the 1930s deepened, so did his desire to preserve its integrity. He became increasingly cautious, determined to minimize his impact and leave as little trace of his presence as possible.

The issue becomes even more complex when venturing further back in time. Though the 1930s posed challenges—limited infrastructure, conservative norms—it was still a recognizable world. But as seen in **Retrorsum Books Two and Three**, where Will and Charles travel to earlier eras, the dangers increase sharply.

In periods like the 1830s or colonial times, modern devices aren't just unusual—they're incomprehensible. A glowing screen or synthetic ringtone might provoke fear, suspicion, or accusations of sorcery. Without electricity or familiar concepts like batteries, these devices are harder to maintain, let alone conceal.

Even practical concerns mount: dust, moisture, and extreme temperatures can easily destroy sensitive electronics. In harsher, more primitive environments, durability and power access become serious limitations. In such cases, Will and Charles relied on solar chargers—but even those presented problems: limited sunlight, slow charging, and the risk of drawing unwanted curiosity from locals.

In the end, the decision to carry 21st-century technology into the past isn't merely about convenience—it's about survival, discretion, and strategic foresight. While the early 1930s may permit the discreet use of modern gear, the further back one travels, the higher the stakes become. The deeper into the past you go, the greater the need for caution, adaptability, and a keen awareness of your surroundings. A misplaced device or an ill-timed use of technology could attract suspicion—or worse.

Bringing 21st-century technology to the early 1930s involves more than just hardware—the data on those devices may be the most valuable asset of all. Laptops or tablets loaded with historical information, maps, etiquette guides, and survival tips could be critical for blending in, staying safe, and navigating daily life.

Access to future sports outcomes—baseball, boxing, horse racing—offers discreet, lucrative opportunities during the Great Depression. In an era where steady income was scarce, such knowledge could mean the difference between hardship and comfort. However, any use of this data must be subtle to avoid suspicion or altering history.

Beyond practical strategy, personal media like music or films can help combat the emotional toll of a long-term presence in a distant past. Revisiting familiar songs or favorite movies offers psychological relief—small but powerful comforts that maintain a sense of normalcy.

Used wisely, 21st-century knowledge can turn a difficult era into one of resilience and adaptability. For a prepared traveler, information isn't just power—it's survival.

Bringing Other Items in the 1930s: Practicality and Risk

When traveling to the early 1930s, the risks of bringing 21st-century items go far beyond obvious electronics. Even everyday objects—like toothpaste tubes, plastic toothbrushes, or modern pill bottles—can raise suspicion due to unfamiliar materials, branding, or packaging. What seems ordinary to a modern traveler might appear strange or alarming in a time with no context for synthetic plastics or advanced pharmaceuticals. A discarded shampoo bottle or labeled container could draw unwanted attention and potentially disrupt efforts to blend in.

To minimize these risks, travelers should use discretion: transfer toiletries into plain, unmarked containers and/or prioritize period-appropriate versions whenever possible. Comfort must be balanced with the need to preserve historical authenticity.

Electronics pose even greater challenges. In Retrorsum: Book One, Will Patterson uses a step-down converter and power bank to safely charge his devices—critical tools for avoiding the dangers of plugging modern tech into unstable 1930s electrical systems. Voltage mismatches, irregular frequency standards, and unreliable infrastructure could easily fry sensitive equipment. In many rural areas, electricity was unreliable or nonexistent.

Adapters for outlet compatibility are also essential, as modern plugs won't fit older sockets. Without proper adapters and converters, even the most valuable tech—loaded with critical data—becomes useless.

Beyond technology, health supplies are vital. In an era with limited medical care, even small injuries can escalate. Antibiotic ointments, general pain relievers, and basic first aid supplies should always be included. As Will does in ***Retrorsum***, carrying a small antibiotic regimen can turn a potential crisis into a manageable inconvenience.

Ultimately, every item brought into the past should be weighed carefully—not just for utility, but for its potential to disrupt or reveal. Smart packing can mean the difference between successful immersion and disastrous exposure.

Blending In and Staying Funded: Survival Strategies for the Past

Blending into the era is essential for any time traveler—especially in a highly visible setting like 1930s Las Vegas. A mismatched outfit can raise suspicion fast, making proper attire one of the most critical early considerations. Dressing in period-appropriate clothing not only helps avoid scrutiny but signals respect for the culture and ensures smoother interactions.

In **Retrorsum: Book One**, Will Patterson initially attempted to blend in with a pair of "Black and Whites" from a vintage store in the present day. Though passable, it wasn't ideal. First impressions mattered in the 1930s, and Will would have benefited from placing more emphasis on his appearance. Still, his decision to shop locally on Fremont Street shortly after arrival was a smart one. Acquiring clothing within the era not only helped him match the local style more accurately but also provided valuable cultural insight—and made his experience feel more authentic.

The same logic applies to money. Acquiring 1930s currency in the 21st century is costly. Coins like Peace Dollars, Buffalo Nickels, and Mercury Dimes, as well as vintage banknotes, are highly collectible today and sell for far more than face value. For example, a single Peace Dollar—worth $1 in 1931—might fetch hundreds or even thousands of dollars in the present, depending on condition and date. While it's wise to carry enough authentic currency to cover the first month or two, a long-term traveler must plan to generate income once in the era.

One practical and discreet method—popularized in fiction and films—is leveraging future knowledge to place calculated bets. This approach was especially effective in 1930s Las Vegas, where sports betting was quasi-legal and the gambling landscape was still forming. In **Retrorsum**, Will used PDFs of **The Las Vegas Age** to track future outcomes of major events like the 1931 World Series, the Kentucky Derby, and headline boxing matches. With this foresight, he placed strategic wagers and established a steady, low-profile income during the height of the Great Depression.

Compared to seeking traditional employment—scarce and competitive in that era—this method offered financial independence and freedom. It allowed Will to immerse himself in 1930s life without being weighed down by the economic struggles of the time. For any time traveler, thoughtful preparation, discretion, and resourcefulness are essential—not only to survive in the past, but to thrive in it as well.

Temporal Sickness & Health Issues

Temporal Sickness: Understanding and Managing Side Effects of Time Travel:

Before delving into other health-related concerns, it is essential to address a common issue faced by temporal visitors: temporal sickness. Often, depending on the method by which a temporal visitor arrives, one may experience bouts of this unsettling condition. The exact cause of temporal sickness remains elusive, but it appears to result from the strain of passing through temporal distortion fields or enduring other unknown factors associated with time travel. These factors can induce a range of symptoms, including nausea, dizziness, headaches, and even occasional vomiting, leaving travelers feeling disoriented and uncomfortable.

Understanding Temporal Sickness:

Temporal sickness is akin to severe motion sickness, but specifically triggered by the unique stresses of moving through different time periods. The dissonance between temporal energies and the traveler's physiology can disrupt normal bodily functions, leading to the aforementioned symptoms. While the exact mechanisms are not fully understood, it is hypothesized that the rapid shift in temporal coordinates affects the nervous system, causing these adverse reactions.

Managing Temporal Sickness:

The most effective method for managing temporal sickness is **rest and recuperation**. If symptoms arise, it is advisable to:

1. **Stay Indoors:** Remain in your hotel room or place of residence. A stable, controlled environment can help mitigate the effects of temporal distortion.
2. **Hydrate and Nourish:** Ensure you stay well-hydrated and consume light, easily digestible foods to support your body's recovery.
3. **Limit Movement:** Avoid strenuous activities and excessive movement, which can exacerbate dizziness and nausea.
4. **Use Remedies:** Over-the-counter medications for motion sickness, such as **dimenhydrinate** or **meclizine**, may provide temporary relief. However, consult with a healthcare provider familiar with temporal travel for personalized recommendations.(**Assuming these ailments are addressed in your home century**)
5. **Stay Calm:** Stress and anxiety can intensify symptoms. Practice deep-breathing exercises or meditation to maintain a sense of calm.

These symptoms typically subside within **48 hours**, allowing the traveler to resume normal activities without lingering effects.

Case Study: Will Patterson in *Retrorsum*

In ***Retrorsum: Book One***, Will Patterson suffered intense nausea and headaches from temporal sickness soon after arriving in 1930s Las Vegas. By resting and avoiding exertion, he gradually recovered—showing that while the condition is disruptive, it can be managed with care and patience.

General Health Issues-Precautions:

As with any trip, maintaining good health is essential—and this becomes even more critical when journeying into the past. Few things can derail an experience faster than illness, especially when traveling to an era like the early 1930s, where medical care is limited and modern treatments are often unavailable.

In that time, many diseases now easily treatable—such as pneumonia, strep throat, or even infected cuts—can become life-threatening. Vaccines and antibiotics are scarce or nonexistent, and sanitation standards vary widely. A minor injury or foodborne illness can quickly escalate. Preparation is crucial: travelers should carry a compact medical kit stocked with antiseptic cream, pain relievers, and a limited supply of antibiotics. Practicing good hygiene and being cautious with food and water are also essential in mitigating risk.

Mental health should not be overlooked either. The stress of adapting to a different era, along with the constant need for discretion, can take a psychological toll. Familiar comforts like books or music from your own time can help maintain emotional stability during prolonged stays.

In ***Retrorsum: Book One***, Will Patterson falls gravely ill with pneumonia in December 1931. Lacking access to proper medical care, he relies on a small supply of antibiotics brought from the present—originally prescribed to his roommate. Though not ordinarily recommended, this decision saves his life. Without those medications, Will would have likely passed, as many did during the Great Depression from what we now consider treatable infections.

This near-tragedy underscores the importance of preparedness. Pneumonia, tuberculosis, and sepsis are serious threats in an era without modern antibiotics, which won't be widely available until the 1940s. Even today, pneumonia can be fatal in high-risk individuals. In 1931, it is far worse.

Will's experience is a sobering reminder: even the best-prepared traveler is vulnerable. A well-stocked medical kit is not just helpful—it can be lifesaving. In a time when illness means rest and hope at best, carrying modern medicine can mean the difference between recovery and disaster.

Travelers to 1930s Las Vegas should prepare for the absence of modern conveniences. The summer of 1931 is among the hottest on record, and air conditioning is almost unheard of. The Apache Hotel's air-conditioned lobby, added in 1932, is a rare luxury. Most cooling relies on swamp coolers—effective only in low humidity and often noisy, unreliable, or insufficient for extreme heat.

Winter brings its own discomforts. November 1931 sees cold winds and even snow. In **Retrorsum: Book One,** Will Patterson falls ill during this period, with a simple cold escalating to pneumonia—an example of how unforgiving the environment can be.

Buildings offer little relief. Most are poorly insulated, making them drafty in winter and suffocating in summer. Heating is often limited to small stoves or basic radiators. Plumbing is rudimentary, with shared bathrooms, low water pressure, and occasional cold-only water taps in more modest accommodations. Hot showers are a luxury, not a guarantee.

Mattresses are thin, lumpy, and stuffed with cotton or horsehair. Linens are scratchy by today's standards. Electric lighting is dim and uneven, and rooms lack reliable outlets or switches. Many hotels and boarding houses have no telephones in rooms—if a phone is available at all, it is shared and located in the lobby.

Food preservation and storage are also limited. Refrigerators are rare; most homes use iceboxes, and food spoils more easily, especially in the desert heat. Ice deliveries are routine, and drinking water is not always safe without boiling.

Even simple things like toilet paper, tissues, or deodorant are either coarse, unavailable, or not yet common. Shaving, hair care, and general grooming require time, effort, and tolerance for rougher tools and products. (In *Retrorsum* Book One, Will Patterson resorted mostly to shaving salons for his hair-trimming needs.)

Understanding these limitations is crucial. With the right clothing, knowledge of local practices, and a realistic mindset, travelers can adapt—but comfort comes from preparedness, not convenience.

Ethical Considerations

Beyond gear and checklists, time travel raises deeper questions—ones that go far beyond the typical sci-fi trope of "changing the timeline." Any serious temporal traveler must confront the ethical implications of bringing advanced knowledge into a less developed era.

One critical question: **Does traveling to the past amount to a form of modern exploitation or soft colonialism?** Armed with superior information and technology, does the traveler gain an unfair—and possibly unethical—advantage? And even if the changes seem harmless, is it right to benefit from a historical context that can't consent or defend itself?

In ***Retrorsum: Book One***, Will Patterson approaches these dilemmas with a mix of practicality and caution. He leverages future knowledge to place discreet bets on events like the 1931 World Series and the 1932 Kentucky Derby, securing his financial comfort while staying at the Gateway Hotel. Will avoids tampering with major events, choosing personal survival over historical disruption.

But even this restrained approach raises difficult questions. Is it ever truly harmless to exploit the past, even subtly? Using insider knowledge may not shift history in obvious ways, but it still reflects a power imbalance—a quiet manipulation of a world unaware of its future.

Time travel, then, is not just a logistical or survival challenge. It's a moral test. A journey into the past demands not only preparation, but self-awareness—a willingness to weigh personal benefit against the integrity of the era being visited. In the end, how a traveler behaves may reveal more about their character than any gadget they carry.

Cultural Shock and Moral Dissonance

Beyond ethical concerns, time travelers must prepare for deep cultural dissonance. The norms and values of a past era—particularly the early 1930s—often starkly contrast with modern sensibilities. Concepts like political correctness, gender equality, and social progressivism will be absent, and their absence will become quickly, and often painfully, obvious.

The 1930s were defined by rigid social hierarchies shaped by race, gender, and class. Racism and segregation were embedded in everyday life, especially under Jim Crow laws. Even in a young Las Vegas, these dynamics shaped housing, employment, and social access. Black workers on the Boulder Dam project, for example, faced wage discrimination and were relegated to distant, underserved communities.

Popular media and advertising echoed the prejudices of the time, often presenting messaging that would shock modern sensibilities. Adapting to this cultural landscape requires care—speaking too freely about civil rights or gender equality could draw suspicion or even hostility, and while the desire to express or even preach such 21st-century values may sound ethical, it is best to understand that the 1930s is far removed from many of the commonly held values of the 21st century or beyond. Discretion and extreme caution are advised.

Social expectations also differ drastically. The lack of modern communication tools, formal etiquette, and restrictive gender roles can feel alienating. Even small details—like table manners or reliance on handwritten letters—demand patience and adaptation.

In short, cultural shock in the 1930s may rival any logistical or ethical challenge. Successfully navigating the past requires not just historical knowledge, but emotional resilience and self-awareness. For the unprepared traveler, the gap between modern identity and historical reality can be just as jarring as the act of time travel itself.

As depicted in **_Retrorsum_**, Will Patterson's arrival near Las Vegas on June 20, 1931, underscores the importance of immediate post-arrival planning. After crossing temporal boundaries, securing your return site is critical—failure to do so could leave you permanently stranded in the past.

Will's approach was simple but effective. Upon his arrival in 1931, he removed the old rags from under his overalls that he used for protection, he then piled desert stones over them to create a makeshift marker—one that would survive the desert environment for some time. He also used his smartphone to take multiple photos of the horizon and nearby landmarks, providing visual cues for locating the arrival upon his intended return.

Creating a durable marker should be a top priority. Stack rocks or dig a shallow trench to create a physical reference point. Use materials that blend with the era but will hold up over time.

Identify fixed local landmarks such as roads, rivers, or unique terrain features. These broader orientation points are useful if your marker is disturbed or the immediate area changes.

Revisit the site periodically if your stay in the target year spans months or even years. Regular visits will keep the area familiar and will help you detect any natural or human interference that may have occurred since your arrival.

Will's method combined modern tools with low-tech backup—an ideal balance. Any time traveler would be wise to adopt a similar strategy. The success of your return may depend entirely on how well you prepare the moment you arrive.

Las Vegas Revealed: Gateway Hotel

[1]

Will Patterson and the Gateway Hotel

Will Patterson's stay at the Gateway Hotel from June 1931 to May 1932 is a pivotal part of **Retrorsum**, offering a firsthand view of 1930s Las Vegas through the eyes of a 21st-century traveler. The hotel, which Will had carefully researched before departure, became more than just a place to stay—it served as a sanctuary during his earliest months in the past.

Its quiet location, just off the bustling Fremont Street, provided the peace and privacy Will needed to reflect and plan. The 24-hour

Gateway Café below offered not only convenient meals but also a sense of immersion in the rhythms of everyday life in Depression-era Nevada.

Will's reflections on his accommodations underscore the importance of selecting the right base of operations. Originally intended as a short-term solution, the Gateway became essential. As the city filled with workers seeking jobs on the Boulder Dam project, vacancies were scarce. Trusting the hotel's security became critical, especially as Will carried sensitive technology and data. The risk of theft—or exposure—was always present, and the Gateway offered enough stability to ease those concerns.

His extended stay there highlights a key lesson for any time traveler: comfort, security, and strategic location matter as much as historical accuracy. Will's experience at the Gateway is not just practical—it adds texture and realism to the narrative, painting a vivid picture of Las Vegas at a turning point in its history.

Alternative Accommodations in 1931-1932 Las Vegas

Apache Hotel:

Opened on March 19, 1932, the Apache Hotel at 130 Fremont Street quickly became the most luxurious hotel in Southern Nevada. Built by P.O. Silvagni, an Italian immigrant and Boulder Dam contractor, it was intended as a retreat for workers but evolved into a hotspot for celebrities like Lucille Ball and Humphrey Bogart.

For time travelers, the Apache offers rare 1930s-era luxuries: the first electric elevator in Las Vegas and an air-conditioned lobby—a major relief during the desert summer. While modest by modern standards, these amenities were cutting-edge at the time. The hotel also featured a café, small shops, and the Apache Indian Village Nightclub.

Sal Sagev Hotel:

Located at Fremont and Main, the Sal Sagev (formerly the Nevada Hotel) was renamed in 1931 after a major renovation—its name, a reversal of "Las Vegas." Known as the city's oldest hotel, it offered central convenience and modest comfort complete with private bathrooms.

Room rates at the time were likely **\$2–3 per day**, and the hotel included a small casino and café. In the decades to come, it would become the Golden Gate Hotel and Casino, but in 1931, it remaines a newly polished cornerstone of Fremont Street.

Overland Hotel:

Directly across from the Sal Sagev, the Overland Hotel offered **slightly larger rooms**, private bathrooms, and similar amenities including a small casino and café. Its comfort and location made it a solid alternative for time travelers needing privacy and accessibility.

• • • •

Northern Club:

Next to the Sal Sagev, the Northern Club was known primarily as a bar and gambling spot. Though it had rooms upstairs in the 1920s, it's unclear if they remained available by 1931. Room rates likely ranged from $1.50–$2 per night.

A safe haven for a drink during Prohibition, the club discreetly served whiskey and spirits. While food wasn't available, cafés like the Las Vegas Café and Oasis Café were nearby—and frequently visited by Will Patterson in Retrosum.

Union and Lincoln Hotels:

Located on South Main Street, the **Union Hotel (227 S. Main)** and **Lincoln Hotel (307 S. Main)** offered simple, no-frills accommodations. The Lincoln's "Old West" design and upper-floor balcony gave it rustic appeal, though both lacked modern comforts.

In ***Retrorsum Book Two***, Charles Damron briefly stayed at the Lincoln before relocating to the more refined Hotel Nevada. Budget-conscious travelers might find these practical, if basic, options.

The Meadows Resort and Casino

Opened in May 1931, The Meadows was located near modern-day Fremont and East Charleston. Operated by bootleggers Frank and Louis Cornero, it quickly gained a reputation for imported liquor and exclusivity during Prohibition.

In the first week of September 1931, a fire broke out in the resort's kitchen, damaging key parts of the property, including their rooms. Despite the setback, the casino remained operational for a time, allowing the venue to continue serving guests.

Though relatively short-lived, The Meadows earned a lasting reputation as a favored destination for Las Vegas high society during its brief but vibrant run.

Colorado Auto Court:

Situated on the 700 block of South 5th Street (later the Las Vegas Strip), the Colorado Auto Court offered a more private stay. Individual heated cabins provided a peaceful retreat from Fremont Street—a prototype for the motor motels of the future.

Its location and layout made it a tranquil option for temporal travelers seeking distance from downtown noise and keeping a low profile.

Disclaimer:

While there are undoubtedly other accommodation options available in 1931-1932 Las Vegas, the establishments listed above are the most notable and well-documented. If you choose to stay at a private residence or rent an apartment, it is crucial to prioritize security, particularly if you are carrying technology or other items from the 21st century. Ensuring the safety of such items is vital, as their loss or discovery could pose significant risks, both to your personal mission and to the integrity of the timeline. Consider your surroundings carefully and select accommodations that provide the privacy and security necessary for a successful temporal visit.

Eateries, Cafes, and Restaurants

A Word About Food in the Early 1930s:

While café and restaurant meals in the 1930s may resemble those of today, home cooking was often far more austere. Most families couldn't afford to eat out or purchase meats and pricier ingredients, making daily meals a test of creativity and resourcefulness.

Sandwiches were common, filled with whatever was on hand—mayonnaise, lard, onion, or even sugar. Dishes like toast with mashed potatoes and gravy or canned tomatoes over bread were cheap and filling. Soups were stretched with water and basic ingredients, such as beans or potatoes. Salads might include foraged dandelion greens.

Breakfasts typically featured cornmeal mush, porridge, or cornbread soaked in milk. Fried staples like potatoes, hot dogs, or bologna were common when meat was available. Protein was used sparingly—boiled cabbage flavored with bacon grease, or hard-boiled eggs in white sauce over rice, helped stretch meals further. In more desperate cases, roadkill, squirrel, or gopher might be on the menu, along with chicken feet or fried chicken skin to simulate a full poultry dish.

Desserts, though modest, brought comfort. Water pie, vinegar pie, and baked apples delivered sweetness without expensive ingredients. These meals, though humble, reflected the toughness and ingenuity of Depression-era families—turning scarcity into sustenance.

Cafés and Eateries in 1931-1932 Las Vegas

Despite its relatively small size during this period, Las Vegas offers a remarkable variety of eateries for a town with only 6,000 to 7,000 residents. Some of these establishments stay open 24 hours, catering to the bustling activity of the growing community. Below is a guide to some of the most notable cafés and diners:

Gateway Café:

Located on Main & Stewart Streets and attached to the Gateway Hotel, the Gateway Café is a convenient and reliable choice for temporal visitors. Open 24 hours, it provides a welcoming space for meals at any time of the day or night. Its connection to the Gateway Hotel makes it particularly practical for those staying there, ensuring easy access to refreshments without needing to venture far. Steaks, chops, short orders, and breakfast are served around the clock.

Will Patterson, in **Book 1 of Retrorsum**, spent a lot of time in this café due to its proximity to where he was staying at the Gateway Hotel.

White Spot Café:

Located at 109 Fremont Street, the White Spot Café quickly becomes one of Las Vegas's most popular dining spots after opening in late August 1931. For time travelers arriving before this date, the café doesn't yet exist, but once operational, its central location and friendly atmosphere make it a go-to destination.

With 24-hour service, it's perfect for a quick meal amid the energy of Fremont Street. The café's design—reminiscent of the classic 1950s diner style that would come later—offers a warm, retro charm that feels ahead of its time. The menu is extensive, featuring burgers, steaks, and hearty all-day breakfasts, catering to nearly every appetite.

Whether stopping in for a quick bite or a relaxed meal, the White Spot Café delivers a quintessentially American dining experience that feels both nostalgic and enduring.

Oasis Café:

The Oasis Café, one of Las Vegas's oldest eateries of the era, offers a timeless yet modest charm that makes it a local favorite. Conveniently located next to the Majestic Theatre on Fremont Street, it serves as a dependable spot for both residents and temporal visitors. Known for its consistent service and welcoming atmosphere, the café blends familiarity with a reminder of how much dining culture has changed.

Doubling as a confectionery, the Oasis offers fresh breads, pastries, and a wide array of sweets. From hearty meals to homemade-style cookies and cakes, it caters to both comfort and cravings. Whether stopping in for a bite or picking up a treat, the Oasis Café captures the spirit of 1930s Las Vegas with warmth and simplicity.

Deluxe Café:

Located further up on Fremont Street between 5th and 6th Streets, the Deluxe Café is mildly more upscale than most of the other restaurants listed here. It even serves a few Chinese dishes, though these may seem rather inadequate compared to Chinese cuisine in the 21st century.

Nevertheless, the café offers a wide selection of dishes, from seafood items and steaks to lamb chops. Based on ads for the café in The Las Vegas Age, it is also perfect for holiday meals such as Thanksgiving and Christmas Eve. The Deluxe Café is an ideal choice if you're in 1930s Las Vegas during the holidays.

The Deluxe Café opens around mid to late 1931, so if you attempt to visit before this time, you'll be out of luck. The Deluxe Café is also mentioned in Books 1 and 3 of the Retrorsum series.

Busy Bee Café:

The Busy Bee Café is located on North 1st Street, very close to both the Gateway Hotel and Block 16 (Las Vegas's red-light district). As the name suggests, the place is often bustling with activity and is mentioned in **Books 1 and 4 of the Retrorsum series.**

In a common practice of the early 1930s, local police frequently bring prisoners to this café to feed them before quickly escorting them out to serve more. Nevertheless, this spot is an excellent choice for enjoying the usual café selections. The Busy Bee Café is one of the few places that survives well into the 1950s.

Casinos and Gaming in 1931-1932 Las Vegas, Nevada

[2]

1931: A New Era of Gambling for Las Vegas:

In 1931, Nevada reached a turning point by reintroducing "wide-open" gambling, not legalizing it for the first time—as commonly believed. Gambling had first been legalized in 1869, then banned in 1909 by Progressive reformers. With the Great Depression ravaging the economy, state lawmakers saw a chance to revive commercial gambling to spur financial growth

.

On March 19, 1931, Governor Fred Balzar signed A.B. 98, allowing establishments like saloons and hotels to host house-banked games such as blackjack and craps. Just 12 days later, Clark County issued licenses to eight venues, igniting Las Vegas's casino era.

Early hotspots included the Northern Club, Las Vegas Club, Boulder Club, and Big 4 Club, helping establish Fremont Street as the city's entertainment core. The Big 4 Club, at 112–114 S. First Street, offered slots, blackjack, and craps, and was known for its colorful chips and collectible matchbooks.

Nearby, the Exchange Club, managed by A.T. McCarter, became a favorite for its refined gaming options, including poker and roulette. The Boulder Club, open since 1929, stood out for its modern two-story design and vibrant atmosphere—quickly becoming a Fremont Street staple.

Though modest by today's standards, these early halls lit the fuse for Las Vegas's transformation into a global gaming hub, setting the tone for its rise as a capital of entertainment.

Benefits for the Temporal Visitor

For the temporal traveler, early 1930s Las Vegas offers rare opportunities—especially for those armed with knowledge of future sporting events. As shown in **Retrorsum,** Will Patterson discreetly placed bets at the Las Vegas Club, Rainbow Club, and Boulder Club in 1931 and 1932, taking full advantage of the newly re-legalized gambling scene.

With minimal regulation and a laid-back atmosphere, Las Vegas during this period is ideal for placing quiet, profitable wagers. The Las Vegas Club, located on Fremont Street, provides a straightforward, low-profile entry point for betting, with a no-frills setup and reliable staff.

The Rainbow Club offers an even more relaxed environment, attracting both locals and visitors—perfect for blending in while gaming. Meanwhile, the Boulder Club, one of the city's first licensed venues, stands out for its energy and variety, catering to a rougher but lively crowd with sports betting and table games.

Advice for Temporal Visitors:

To make the most of your visit, it's essential to understand the gambling culture and social etiquette of 1930s Las Vegas. Unlike today's polished casinos, venues of this era are more personal and intimate. Dress smartly and in period-appropriate attire to avoid unwanted attention and blend in naturally.

If you're placing bets using knowledge of future events, discretion is critical. Oversight may be minimal, but acting too confidently—or drawing attention with anachronistic insights—can raise suspicion. Make sure you're familiar with the sports, teams, and terminology of the time. Any sign of unfamiliarity could alert locals or bookies.

Above all, immerse yourself in the atmosphere. Early 1930s Las Vegas is more than a betting ground—it's a city on the brink of transformation. Stroll Fremont Street, engage with locals, and take in the mix of grit, charm, and opportunity that defines this pivotal era. For the time traveler, the experience itself is far more valuable than any winnings.

Prohibition, Drinking & Alcohol in Early 1930s Las Vegas

1931 and 1932 marked the final full years of Prohibition in the United States. While illegal alcohol still flowed, enforcement efforts in places like Las Vegas intensified—though largely without success.

The tide began to turn in March 1933, when President Franklin D. Roosevelt signed the Cullen–Harrison Act, allowing the sale of beer and wine up to 3.2% alcohol. The law took effect on April 7, later celebrated as National Beer Day. By December 5, 1933, Prohibition officially ended with the ratification of the 21st Amendment.

In early 1931, Las Vegas authorities opened a speakeasy called **"Liberty's Last Stand"** near Block 16 and the Gateway Hotel. Secretly ran by federal dry agents, it served as a sting operation to expose bootlegging networks, leading to multiple raids—underscoring the tension between enforcement and the city's booming underground alcohol trade.

Caution: Drinking During Prohibition:

For temporal visitors, Las Vegas in 1931–1932 offers the allure of Prohibition-era nightlife—but it comes with serious risks. While the end of Prohibition is near, enforcement remains active and, in some areas, more aggressive than ever. Complacency is dangerous.

Block 16, known for its illegal saloons and speakeasies, may tempt visitors seeking an authentic prohibition-era experience, but these venues were often under surveillance by local or federal agents. Raids were common, and arrests could expose travelers to violence, criminal elements, or legal jeopardy.

Las Vegas at the time was filled with outlaws, swindlers, and opportunists thriving in the chaos. While some may seem harmless, many were desperate and predatory. Speakeasies may seem charming and historically rich, but the risks of arrest and exposure can potentially outweigh the thrill.

The greatest danger lies in being detained by law enforcement. Arrest could lead to the search of your accommodations under loose legal standards. Protections like due process and search warrants were inconsistently applied—especially for suspected bootleggers. Any discovery of modern items—phones, tools, or even packaging—could provoke intense scrutiny. Such findings would be impossible to explain within 1930s logic and could risk revealing the very existence of time travel.

The social climate only increases the threat. Police often worked with federal agents, and suspects were routinely intimidated or coerced during interrogation. Even a minor infraction could escalate quickly.

To stay safe:

1. Be mindful of "locals" advice regarding raids
2. Never bring any modern gadgets or items to speakeasies, theft can be common.
3. Use local resources, if possible, like the *Las Vegas Age* newspaper to check for raids before visiting establishments (checking the *Las Vegas Age*, dated a day after an intended visit, as many raids often make the news).

· · · ·

As **Retrorsum: Book One** highlights, Will Patterson understood the stakes. He feared even a small misstep could unravel everything. Being forced to explain 21st-century technology to a Prohibition-era officer would be a catastrophic breach—the ultimate nightmare for any time traveler.

Speakeasys and Drinking Esablishments of 1931 Las Vegas:

[3]

The Desert Inn Nightclub, not to be confused with Wilbur Clark's 1950s casino of the same name, holds a unique place in Las Vegas history as one of the few—possibly the only—Black-owned businesses operating downtown during the early 1930s. Amid deeply entrenched segregation, its existence is both remarkable and significant.

Though historical records are limited, some suggest a gaming license is issued in 1931 to a Black entrepreneur—a rare achievement for the time. The club likely serves as both an entertainment venue and a community hub for Black residents, who are barred from most public spaces. Based on ads from the *The Las Vegas Age*, surely there were white patrons to the establishment as well

In ***Retrorsum: Book One,*** Will Patterson recalls the Desert Inn as a rare place where Black and white patrons mingle freely, defying the era's rigid social divisions. Known for its Southern-inspired cuisine—Virginia baked ham, BBQ chicken, and other comforting favorites—it stands out as a culinary gem. But its soul is in the music:

Southern jazz and crazy blues from the 1920s and '30s fill the air nightly, creating a lively, welcoming atmosphere that draws locals and visitors alike.

For time travelers, this venue offers an unforgettable glimpse into 1930s nightlife, cultural crossover, and resilience. Though not publicly advertised, bootlegged liquor is available, adding an extra layer of Prohibition-era intrigue to this vibrant, historic gem.

Prohibition Drinks and Other Drinking Spots in 1930s Las Vegas:

With few exceptions—namely the Meadows Resort and select higher-tier venues—the quality of alcohol in 1930s Las Vegas varies wildly. While some establishments manage to serve passable spirits, much of the liquor is barely drinkable and sometimes outright dangerous. Poorly distilled batches can lead to poisoning or serious health risks.

Block 16 speakeasies are particularly infamous for their questionable booze. Many operate on thin margins, prioritizing quantity over quality. A common offering is *bathtub gin*—a harsh, unrefined liquor made in unsanitary, makeshift stills. Taste and safety are secondary; getting drunk is the primary goal.

Drinking this kind of liquor is itself a gamble. The burning taste and unpredictable effects are legendary, with even regulars complaining about the flavor. Still, the combination of strong drinks and the thrill of the speakeasy keeps patrons coming back.

In contrast, venues like the Meadows Resort offer imported or better-crafted spirits, catering to a more refined clientele and evoking a sense of pre-Prohibition luxury—though such places are rare in a city still shaping its identity.

For the temporal visitor, the message is clear: indulge with caution. Knowing where you're drinking—and what you're drinking—can make the difference between a memorable night and a regrettable one.

In ***Retrorsum: Book One***, Will Patterson frequents a range of establishments, including the Meadows Resort, the roadside Blue Heaven en route to Boulder City, and the Red Rooster and Pair "O" Dice along the LA Highway (now The Strip). These venues often double as respectable restaurants by day, serving alcohol of varying quality after dark.

The Northern Club on Fremont Street is a dependable spot to get whiskey, purported to be better than average for the era. Will, in ***Book One of Retrorsum***, notes that the Northern Club is one of the "safer" spots to have a drink, as it is one of the main establishments on Fremont Street. Unlike the joints on Block 16, the Northern Club appears to be free from the raids that are an ever-present reality for establishments in that district.

[4]

Other Entertainment Options in 1930s Las Vegas

Beyond its casinos, speakeasies, and cafés, 1930s Las Vegas also offers a modest but vibrant theater scene, serving as a cultural escape for locals and temporal visitors alike.

The El Portal Theater, opened in 1928 on Fremont Street, stands as the crown jewel of the city's cinemas. Built in the Spanish Colonial Revival style, it is the first building in Las Vegas with air cooling, offering a welcome break from the desert heat. With seating for around 700, El Portal showcases both late silent films and early talkies in an elegant, atmospheric setting—making it a top destination for cinematic magic.

Just off Carson Street, the Airdome Theater offers a more rustic experience. As one of Las Vegas's earliest theaters, this open-air venue is popular in summer, screening silent films and early sound pictures beneath the stars. Its simple setup provides a charming glimpse into the pioneering days of cinema.

Next door to the Oasis Café, the Majestic Theater caters to live performance lovers. Hosting local plays and small productions, it offers a more intimate alternative to film—reflecting the city's early artistic spirit and providing cultural variety for the curious traveler.

Finally, the Palace Theater, which opens in May 1932 on South 2nd Street, brings a touch of modernity. With a sleek design and regular showings of popular films, it quickly becomes a favorite spot for Depression-era audiences seeking both escapism and entertainment.

These theaters, each with its own character, reflect the vibrant cultural landscape of 1930s Las Vegas. Whether drawn to the grandeur of the El Portal, the open-air charm of the Airdome, or the intimacy of the Majestic and Palace, time travelers find these venues offer a vivid window into the city's evolving artistic identity.

For outdoor leisure, Lorenzi Lake Park is a top destination during the early 1930s. Originally developed by French immigrant David G. Lorenzi, who purchases the land in 1912, the park officially opens in 1926 and quickly becomes a popular retreat for locals and visitors.

Featuring a dance pavilion, swimming pool, scenic lakes, and orchards, Lorenzi Park offers a welcome escape from the desert heat. The pavilion hosts lively dances with the music of the era, while the serene lakes and shaded groves make it a favorite for picnics, fishing, and family outings.

Amid the rough edges of a still-developing city, Lorenzi Lake Park stands out as a rare oasis of relaxation and refinement, capturing the spirit of a community embracing leisure, nature, and culture during the rise of Las Vegas.

Becoming Closer to Locals: Love, Romance, or Close Friendship

One of the most delicate challenges facing any time traveler is the risk of becoming romantically or emotionally involved with someone native to the era—especially in a period like the early 1930s. As with any journey into uncharted territory, emotional connections can complicate what was meant to be a detached exploration.

Human needs—companionship, love, connection—don't vanish just because you've crossed time. As Will Patterson learns in **Retrorsum: Book One**, the longer one remains in the past, the more present and real it becomes. What begins as curiosity can easily grow into genuine attachment, especially when faced with isolation from your own time.

But such connections come with consequences. The 1930s' social roles, gender expectations, and family dynamics differ significantly from modern norms. A romance, however innocent, can alter someone's life path—and potentially the historical timeline itself.

To avoid unintended impact, set clear emotional boundaries before your journey. Recognize that feelings of longing may arise from temporal displacement, not genuine compatibility. Approach each relationship—romantic or platonic—with care, empathy, and restraint.

Forging a connection in another era may seem comforting, even inevitable. But it's vital to weigh that comfort against your moral and temporal responsibilities. Will's story serves as a reminder: your role is to observe, not interfere. Manage your solitude with foresight, not impulse.

The next section offers practical steps and strategies to help avoid or mitigate these risks. Caution and self-awareness are essential when navigating the emotional terrain of the past.

Suggestions for Navigating Emotional Involvement as a Time Traveler

1. Recognize the Historical Context:

Understand the socio-economic context and social dynamics of your target era. During the Great Depression, for instance, sudden income loss, shifting gender roles, and rising marital tensions were common. Awareness of these patterns helps you interpret behavior without projecting modern assumptions.

2. Consider the Impact of Emotional Bonds:

Forming close relationships—romantic, friendly, or familial—can unintentionally influence local decisions and disrupt social dynamics. Even small gestures, like giving advice or financial help, may alter family finances, social roles, or parenting approaches, subtly reshaping the historical narrative you aimed to observe, not change.

3. Balance Empathy with Non-Interference:

Empathy is natural, but remember—you are an outsider in their timeline. Too much involvement risks distorting historical authenticity. Aim to be a sympathetic observer, not a problem-solver. Your role is not to fix the past, but to understand it without interference.

4. Maintain an Observational Stance:

To protect historical continuity, set clear personal boundaries. Avoid sharing future knowledge or introducing ideas and technologies not yet discovered—these can distort cultural development and influence key life decisions. If questioned about your background, offer neutral, era-appropriate explanations that conceal your temporal origin.

5. Assess the Consequences of Revealing Your Identity:

Revealing your identity as a time traveler can trigger disbelief, panic, or attempts to exploit your knowledge. You may be seen as a threat, a resource, or a curiosity. Before disclosing anything, weigh the ethical and emotional consequences. In most cases, it's safer—for both you and the timeline—to maintain your cover and remain inconspicuous.

6. Contemplate the Allure of Staying:

Emotional attachments can tempt you to stay in the target year. Forming bonds with individuals or families may lead to thoughts of "settling down." **In Retrorsum: Book One,** Will Patterson wrestled with this very dilemma. Before making such a choice, carefully consider the consequences:

○ **Psychological Strain:** Adjusting permanently to a past lifestyle without your familiar technologies, values, or social norms can be emotionally taxing.

○ **Ethical Burden:** You may alter future lineages or prevent pivotal historical outcomes by your continued presence.

○ **Practical Challenges:** Securing legal documents, stable income, and acceptance in an era not your own could prove insurmountable. Remember that you are not only changing your life path but also potentially unraveling threads of history.

7. **Rely on Pre-Travel Training and Contingency Plans:**

Before your travel to the past, establish a personal code of conduct. Know how you'll respond to questioning, resist the urge to intervene, and decide what to do if you're tempted to stay. Identify potential "safe havens"—quiet towns or supportive communities—where you can retreat if emotions cloud your judgment. (Remember, the decision to remain in a target year could be a permanent cure to an otherwise very temporary feeling or set of emotions, with no possibility of reversing the effects or returning to your respective home century.)

8. **Document Your Actions and Feelings:**

Document your interactions and emotional responses. After returning to your original time, review moments where you neared disclosure or disrupted social norms. This reflection will help refine your time-travel protocols, allowing you to better balance empathy with historical integrity in future missions.

By following these guidelines, you ensure that your presence in the past remains respectful, minimally invasive, and ethically sound. While meaningful connections with historical individuals are possible, they require careful consideration of potential consequences—both for the people you meet and for the historical continuum you strive to preserve.

Some of the following points may overlap with earlier guidance on relationships, but they bear repeating: numerous factors can prevent a safe return to your original time. You might miss your departure coordinates due to inclement weather, natural disaster, or logistical delays—especially when relying on century-old transportation methods. In **Retrorsum: Book Three**, Will Patterson carefully planned his return from 1839 New Orleans, mindful of the time needed to reach the Providence lab. You must do the same: allow for delays and respect the limitations of the era's infrastructure.

Emotional and psychological barriers can be just as dangerous. Deepening attachments may cause hesitation at the moment of departure—especially if a companion's welfare feels unresolved. Unexpected political unrest or social suspicion can also trap you. Local authorities may restrict movement if your accent, behavior, or possessions raise alarm.

There's also the risk of technical failure or compromise. Your return method—be it a device, recorded vital instructions on what to do in certain predicaments, or many other unforeseen circumstances—could become severely compromised, leading to you being inevitably stranded in the target year.

To prepare, anticipate contingencies:

1. Identify alternate return sites.(If such possibilities are present)
2. Memorize or conceal backup instructions.
3. Maintain a low profile to avoid drawing attention regarding the significance of your return location.
4. Learn basic survival and navigation techniques relevant to the era.
5. Practice plausible cover stories for detentions or

interrogations.

If needed, build trust with a local, but remember—emotional entanglements carry risk.

In the end, no amount of planning can eliminate all variables. But with resilience, flexibility, and foresight, you can reduce the chances of being permanently stranded—and better manage the unknowns of temporal travel.

Preparing Vital Data: A Lifeline for Stranded Time Travelers

In the **Retrorsum series (Books One through Three)**, Nick Patel insisted that any time traveler—no matter how brief the journey—be prepared for permanent stranding. He understood that even a minor error, like missing a rendezvous or encountering a malfunction, could make return impossible. To mitigate this, he developed a rigorous protocol to help travelers sustain themselves indefinitely in the past.

Central to this plan was the provision of future knowledge, especially a detailed record of sports outcomes. By placing strategic bets on known events, travelers could secure a steady income, avoiding reliance on menial labor or unstable employment of the era. This "insurance policy" of critical data allowed them to maintain financial stability, blend in socially, and avoid the hardships of pre-modern life.

All future data should be stored in two formats: digitally (on a secure laptop or tablet) and physically (in a small, concealable notebook). Devices must be protected by strong passwords or biometric locks to prevent unauthorized access (though this may be considered unnecessary considering the time periods mentioned, and a simple 4-digit password would suffice). In case of technical failure or confiscation, the paper backup ensures continued access to vital information.

To avoid detection, the written archive should be disguised—using shorthand, symbols, or coded references only the traveler would understand. This protects the content even if the notebook falls into local hands.

As shown in **Retrorsum: Book One**, Will Patterson carried only the specific data he needed for betting—baseball stats, horse races, etc.—never the full archive. The main notebook always remained safely in his room to prevent loss or theft.

This level of preparation transforms a potential disaster into a manageable scenario, allowing stranded travelers to survive—and even thrive—despite being decades or centuries from home.

Reminder! Personal Security and Safety in Early 1930s Las Vegas:

Although this topic has been addressed previously, the following advice and protocols are essential to ensure both the safety of the temporal traveler and the security of their possessions while residing in a given era. Every measure—from careful data management to strategic discretion—helps guard against theft, damage or other complications.

Surviving the Shadows: Navigating 1930s Las Vegas

At this time, Las Vegas was not yet the entertainment capital it would become. It was a small, rapidly changing town shaped by the economic and social upheavals of Prohibition. Bootleggers and criminal elements operated openly. Violent crimes, including unsolved murders tied to alcohol rackets, were common. Tensions were high as law enforcement struggled to maintain order amid corruption, illicit deals, and shifting alliances. Rumors of paid-off police, deadly rivalries, and speakeasy bombings created an atmosphere of danger and distrust.

For the temporal traveler, 1930s Las Vegas presents distinct hazards. Standing out in dress, speech, or behavior can attract dangerous attention. With desperation and greed prevalent, protecting valuables and maintaining a low profile is vital. Gambling—even on sports—may link the traveler to rival criminal factions. A misplaced question or casual remark could arouse suspicion and spark conflict.

Blending in is essential. Avoid frequenting the same venue, particularly those tied to bootlegging. Keep advanced knowledge of events—gambling outcomes or historical incidents—strictly hidden. Coded notes, as discussed earlier, serve the dual purpose of preserving your edge while avoiding unwanted interest. Rather than rely on modern devices, which may be misunderstood or seized, adopt cover stories grounded in the culture and economy of the time.

In short, navigating early 1930s Las Vegas requires vigilance, discretion, and disciplined information management. With careful planning and caution, even the volatile underworld of Prohibition-era Vegas can be safely navigated.

Case Study: Will Patterson in Retrorsum

In *Retrorsum* **Book One**, Will Patterson initially planned a short stay at the Gateway Hotel while seeking permanent housing. However, familiarity with the staff led him to extend his stay.

Drawing from Will's experience, exercise caution when choosing lodging in 1930s Las Vegas. The era was marked by hidden agendas, unstable alliances, and violent rivalries driven by the illegal liquor trade. Observe who else stays at your hotel or boarding house. Note whether guests appear to be professionals, laborers, or members of the criminal underworld. Watch for discreet exchanges, unusual activity at night, or sudden silences when you approach.

Choose accommodations where the proprietors respect privacy and discourage illicit activity. Ideally, your lodging should attract neither trouble nor curiosity. In a town where suspicion can be dangerous, your residence matters. A stable, inconspicuous base allows you to move safely through the complex social terrain of Prohibition-era Las Vegas.

- **Prohibition-Era Challenges:**

o Open operations of bootleggers and other criminal elements.

o High levels of corruption and violent crimes.

- **Safety Precautions:**

o Secure valuables and conceal personal data.

o Avoid establishing patterns that could attract attention.

- **Strategic Blending:**

o Develop plausible cover stories based on local culture.

o Use data encryption and coded notes to protect sensitive information.

- **Case Study Insights:**

o **Will Patterson**'s extended stay at the **Gateway Hotel** highlights the importance of building trustworthy relationships while maintaining caution.

Tips for Temporal Travelers:

1. **Stay Inconspicuous:** Dress appropriately and adopt local speech patterns to avoid standing out.
2. **Choose Lodging Wisely:** Opt for accommodations that prioritize tenant privacy and have a low profile.

3. **Observe and Adapt:** Pay attention to local behaviors and adjust your actions to fit in seamlessly.
4. **Protect Your Information:** Use passwords, pin codes and avoid sharing sensitive knowledge that could compromise your safety.
5. **Remain Vigilant:** Always be aware of your surroundings and be prepared to react to potential threats swiftly.

By adhering to these guidelines, temporal travelers can enhance their personal security and navigate the complexities of 1930s Las Vegas with greater confidence and safety. While some of the previous tips may seem unnecessary or may not apply to your particular situation, it is important to remain aware and exercise discretion.

Excursions Outside of Las Vegas in 1931-1932

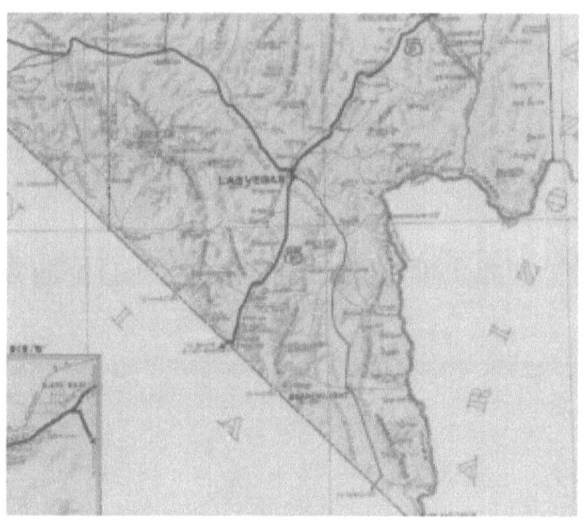

[5]

Travel Guide: Exploring Las Vegas and Beyond in the Early 1930s

Las Vegas in the early 1930s is a quiet, modest town, worlds apart from the bustling metropolis it later becomes. With a population of just a few thousand, the city offers a handful of attractions and a charming small-town atmosphere. For those looking to experience the region in this era, there's more than just the town itself to explore—the surrounding area is full of natural wonders and fascinating sites.

Explore the Mojave Desert:

One of the most remarkable aspects of visiting Las Vegas in 1931 is the chance to step into the unspoiled Mojave Desert that stretches endlessly around the town. Walking less than an hour in any direction from downtown takes you beyond the few paved streets and into a rugged, untouched wilderness. Here, you encounter wide-open skies, rocky landscapes, and hardy desert plants such as creosote bushes and cacti. The air is dry, and the profound silence is broken only by the occasional breeze or the distant call of desert wildlife.

For travelers from any time period, the contrast between Las Vegas's small-town charm and the vast desert is striking. In the absence of modern infrastructure or the artificial glow that defines the 21st century, the desert offers a rare chance to experience a tranquil, timeless setting.

Visit the Boulder Dam Project:

For those seeking an adventure just outside the city, a trip to the Boulder Dam site in nearby Boulder City is a must. The dam—later renamed Hoover Dam—is under construction in 1931 and represents one of the most ambitious engineering projects of the era. Getting there is easy thanks to Boulder City Stages, a local bus line with an office at No. 9 Fremont Street. They offer four daily trips to Boulder City, giving visitors plenty of flexibility to plan their excursion.

The bus ride from Las Vegas to Boulder City takes you through a landscape of stark desert beauty. Along the way, you see the raw Mojave as it exists before mass development, with dry riverbeds and the expansive, rugged terrain that defines the region. It's a picturesque yet rugged journey, perfect for soaking in the atmosphere of the Southwest.

Discover Boulder City:

Boulder City itself is a new settlement, built primarily to house the workers and families involved in the construction of Boulder Dam. In the early 1930s, the town remains under development, with much of its infrastructure and housing appearing temporary or incomplete. Despite this, Boulder City is a hive of activity, offering a fascinating glimpse into the life of workers during one of the Great Depression's largest public works projects.

While the town is utilitarian in design, it reflects the determination and innovation of the era. Don't forget to bring water and a hat, as the desert heat can be intense.

Plan Your Journey:

Whether you're interested in exploring the quiet streets of early Las Vegas, immersing yourself in the vast Mojave Desert, or witnessing history in the making at the Boulder Dam site, this region in the early 1930s has something unique to offer. The combination of natural beauty and human ambition makes it an unforgettable destination for locals, visitors, and even temporal travelers from the future.

Plan your excursions wisely, as travel times are long and amenities are limited compared to the modern era. Bring comfortable(period appropriate) shoes of the time for walking, and don't miss the opportunity to take in the stunning desert views and the historic moments unfolding just outside Las Vegas.

[6]

Broader Horizons: Exploring Southern California and Beyond in the 1930s

For more adventurous temporal explorers—or those embarking on an extended mission to the early 1930s—the region outside Southern Nevada offers a wide variety of travel destinations to suit many interests. The surrounding areas present opportunities to experience dynamic landscapes and cultural hubs of the era, each offering a distinct flavor of early 20th-century life.

Southern California: A Short Journey to Excitement

One of the most accessible and appealing destinations is Southern California, a relatively short journey from Southern Nevada. In the early 1930s, cities like Los Angeles are bustling centers of growth and innovation, offering an incredible range of sights, sounds, and experiences for visitors. The city stands as an epicenter of the film industry during the Golden Age of Hollywood, making it a fascinating destination for anyone intrigued by the glamour and transformation of American entertainment.

In ***Book One of Retrorsum***, Will Patterson, driven by curiosity and a desire to explore a larger urban environment, travels to Los Angeles to experience one of the most vibrant cities in the United States of the time. His journey highlights the city's allure for temporal explorers. From the grand movie palaces lining Broadway to the thriving neighborhoods that reflect the city's diverse population, Los Angeles captures the energy of a rapidly changing America.

What to Expect in 1930s Los Angeles:

For visitors arriving in the early 1930s, Los Angeles offers a mix of old-world charm and modern ambition. The city is growing rapidly, fueled by the booming film industry and advancements in aviation and oil production. Highlights for travelers might include:

- **Hollywoodland:** By the 1930s, Hollywood is already a legendary hub for filmmaking. Visitors can stroll along Hollywood Boulevard or catch a glimpse of a working studio. Though the Walk of Fame and other modern tourist landmarks don't yet exist, the area buzzes with the excitement of the film industry's biggest names and productions.

- **Downtown Los Angeles:** The downtown area is a mix of Art Deco skyscrapers, bustling markets, and cultural landmarks. The recently completed Los Angeles City Hall, an iconic Art Deco structure, stands as the tallest building in the city at the time and is worth a visit.

- **The Beaches:** Southern California's coastline offers a peaceful contrast to the city. In the 1930s, places like Santa Monica and Venice Beach retain much of their charm, with quieter boardwalks and sandy shores ideal for a relaxing day trip.

Accommodation Guide: Where to Stay in Early 1930s Los Angeles

For temporal travelers visiting Los Angeles in the early 1930s, finding the right place to stay is essential to fully experience the charm and energy of the era. From the grandeur of iconic hotels to the historic character of quieter establishments, the city offers a range of accommodations to suit every traveler's taste. Here's a guide to some of the most notable places to stay in 1930s Los Angeles.

The Fremont Hotel:

Location: 401 South Olive Street, Bunker Hill
Style: Mission Revival

The Fremont Hotel, perched on Bunker Hill, is an excellent, but more modest choice for travelers seeking a blend of comfort and stunning views. Opened in 1902, the Fremont boasts a Mission Revival architectural style and approximately 100 well-appointed rooms. Its elevated location offers panoramic vistas of downtown Los Angeles, making it a serene retreat in the heart of the city.

With its proximity to key downtown attractions and its reputation as a distinguished establishment, the Fremont Hotel attracts both tourists and notable figures of the time. If you're a temporal traveler seeking an authentic experience of early 20th-century Los Angeles, this hotel provides a charming and quieter alternative to some of the larger establishments.

Tip: For those interested in exploring historic Bunker Hill, the Fremont's location puts you within walking distance of its unique homes and winding streets, offering a true taste of the neighborhood's character.

The Ambassador Hotel

Location: Wilshire Boulevard (Mid -Wilshire)
Style: Mediterranean Revival

The Ambassador Hotel is one of the crown jewels of 1930s Los Angeles. Opened in 1921, this sprawling luxury hotel on Wilshire Boulevard is renowned for its opulent design, celebrity clientele, and vibrant social scene. It is home to the famous Coconut Grove nightclub, where Hollywood's elite gather to enjoy evenings of entertainment and glamour. If you're looking to immerse yourself in the glitz and excitement of the era, the Ambassador is the place to be.

Accommodations range from luxurious suites to comfortable standard rooms, all designed with elegance and sophistication. The expansive gardens and recreational facilities add a resort-like feel, perfect for those looking to unwind after a day exploring the city.

Tip: Dress your best and make an evening at the Coconut Grove part of your stay—it's a chance to rub shoulders with the stars of the Golden Age of Hollywood and witness world-class performances.

In book one of ***Retrosum***, Will and Antoinette make an evening at the famed Coconut Grove at the Ambassador Hotel in Los Angeles.

The Biltmore Hotel

Location: 506 South Grand Avenue, Downtown Los Angeles
Style: Beaux-Arts
For travelers seeking grandeur and prestige, the Biltmore Hotel in downtown Los Angeles delivers an unforgettable experience. Opened in 1923, this Beaux-Arts masterpiece is considered one of the finest hotels in the country. With over 1,000 rooms, the Biltmore offers unmatched luxury and convenience, making it a favorite among business travelers, Hollywood stars, and visiting dignitaries.

The Biltmore's elegant interior features marble columns, ornate ceilings, and lavish ballrooms, which are frequently used for high-profile events. Its central location puts you close to many downtown attractions, including theaters, museums, and shopping districts.

Tip: Make time to enjoy the Biltmore's grand dining room or afternoon tea service—both provide an excellent opportunity to soak in the ambiance and observe the city's high society in action. Also, the **Palm Room** serves as the unofficial quintessential speakeasy at night.

In Book One of *Retrorsum*, Will has a fateful encounter with Claudia Bianco at the renowned Biltmore Speakeasy, a hidden gem tucked away beneath the grandeur of the iconic Biltmore Hotel. The speakeasy, with its dim lighting, music-filled atmosphere, and an air of forbidden allure, sets the stage for an evening that will leave an indelible mark on Will's journey.

During the night, Will strikes up a conversation with Claudia and her husband, sharing drinks and stories amidst the lively crowd. The highlight of the evening comes when Will takes to the dance floor with Claudia for a life-changing dance. The moment is charged with a mix of elegance, emotion, and an undercurrent of unspoken connection. This transformative experience, against the backdrop of the speakeasy's roaring energy, becomes a pivotal moment in Will's tale, setting into motion a series of events that will ripple throughout his adventure.

Travel Advice for Temporal Visitors:

- Security and Discretion: With the Great Depression bringing economic challenges, be mindful of your possessions and surroundings, especially in crowded hotel lobbies or public areas.

- Blend In: To avoid drawing attention, choose period-appropriate clothing and accessories. While hotels like the Ambassador and the Biltmore cater to wealthier clientele, the staff is accustomed to discretion and will respect your privacy. (Will used this to his advantage)

- Explore Proximity: Each of these hotels is strategically located. The Fremont offers easy access to Bunker Hill's charm, the Ambassador immerses you in the glamour of Wilshire Boulevard, and the Biltmore places you at the heart of downtown Los Angeles across from Pershing Square.

For temporal exploration, these hotels, especially the Biltmore and Ambassador hotels, represent the finest accommodations Los Angeles has to offer in the early 1930s. Each offers its own unique window into the culture, history, and vibrancy of this transformative era.

Travel Logistics for Temporal Explorers

Travel from Southern Nevada to Southern California in the early 1930s typically involves trains or buses. The railroads are well-established by this time, making train travel a comfortable and scenic option for those looking to journey westward. The bus systems also provide affordable and reliable transportation, connecting smaller towns to major urban centers like Los Angeles.

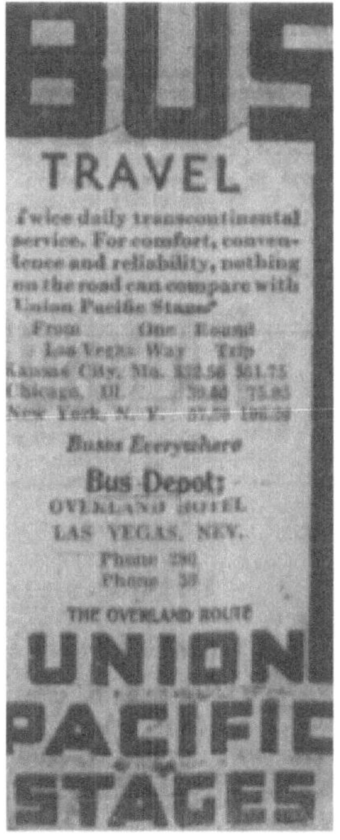

[7]

Travel Guide: Exploring Beyond 1930s Las Vegas by Train

If you're visiting 1930s Las Vegas, **the Union Pacific Station** at Fremont and Main is a must-see. As one of the city's key landmarks, it connects Las Vegas to major cities across the U.S., symbolizing progress in a town still finding its identity.

Where Can You Go?

The Los Angeles Limited, operated by Union Pacific, offers a direct, comfortable route to Los Angeles. Whether you're drawn by Hollywood, urban life, or coastal culture, it's a convenient escape from Nevada. Eastbound, trains reach Salt Lake City, St. Louis, and Chicago, giving travelers a chance to experience iconic American cities during a transformative decade.

A Changing Travel Landscape:

While trains remain dominant in the early 1930s, road and air travel are rapidly emerging. Affordable automobiles and a growing highway network, including Route 66, offer flexibility for adventurous motorists. Bus lines like Greyhound provide intercity service for those without cars.

Air travel, still in its infancy, is gaining prestige. By the mid-1930s, airlines like United and American begin offering scheduled flights—expensive, but a glimpse into the future of travel.

For now, rail travel remains king. Trains offer unmatched comfort, reliability, and reach, making them ideal for both regional trips and cross-country adventures. The Union Pacific Station anchors this network, making it central to any extended exploration.

Union Pacific Buses: Extending the Reach:

Union Pacific also operated Union Pacific Stages, a bus system that filled gaps in rail coverage. By the early 1930s, its fleet of over 200 buses connected places trains couldn't reach, such as Boulder City, a key site during the Boulder Dam construction. Buses also ran to Salt Lake City, Denver, and Los Angeles, offering flexibility for travelers.

During the Great Depression, Union Pacific acquired failed routes, including those from Pickwick-Greyhound. However, the Motor Carrier Act of 1935 restricted expansion to non-parallel rail lines, prompting Union Pacific to integrate bus routes into its passenger service—eventually forming part of Overland Greyhound Lines.

Travel Security in Public Transit: Tips for Temporal Visitors:

In **Retrorsum: Book One**, Will Patterson's caution with 21st-century gear highlights the dangers of travel during the Great Depression. Economic hardship bred theft, swindlers, and opportunists.

Key Tips for Time Travelers:

- **Keep valuables close**. Will never left his gear unattended, even in hotel rooms. Choose secure accommodations, like the Biltmore in Los Angeles, known for respecting guest privacy.

- **Inspect services firsthand**. Will visited train stations to understand luggage handling before traveling—wise, as theft was common.

- **Beware of swindlers**. Avoid overfriendly strangers and dubious offers. Con men and "professionals" offering help were often scammers.

- **Avoid snake oil salesmen**. Traveling salesmen peddled fake cures and gadgets. Will dodged one such scam in Needles, California.

- **Blend in**. Will used a discreet backpack for modern items and stored period-appropriate gear in the train's cargo. Looking inconspicuous reduces curiosity.

- **Be alert in crowds**. Stations and terminals were prime hunting grounds for pickpockets. Stay guarded and keep bags close.

The following compilation presents a generous selection of notable sporting events that took place during the years 1931 and 1932. While it is generally expected that any well-prepared temporal traveler would have thoroughly researched and secured such historical data prior to embarking on their journey, one can never be entirely certain that no crucial details have been overlooked or forgotten. In light of that, what follows may serve as a valuable supplement—a means of filling in any gaps and ensuring that you are well-prepared with the sporting highlights of this particular era.

1931 World Series

- **Teams:** St. Louis Cardinals (NL) vs. Philadelphia Athletics (AL)
- **Series Result:** St. Louis Cardinals won, 4–3

Game-by-Game Results (All 9 Innings):

- **Game 1 (October 1, 1931):** Cardinals 6 – Athletics 2
- **Game 2 (October 2, 1931):** Athletics 2 – Cardinals 0
- **Game 3 (October 4, 1931):** Athletics 5 – Cardinals 2
- **Game 4 (October 5, 1931):** Cardinals 3 – Athletics 1
- **Game 5 (October 6, 1931):** Athletics 5 – Cardinals 1
- **Game 6 (October 7, 1931):** Cardinals 8 – Athletics 2
- **Game 7 (October 10, 1931):** Cardinals 4 – Athletics 2

Noteworthy Detail:

The Cardinals came from behind in the series to claim victory in the decisive seventh game, marking a redemption against the Athletics, who had beaten them the previous year.

1932 World Series

- **Teams:** New York Yankees (AL) vs. Chicago Cubs (NL)
- **Series Result:** New York Yankees won, 4–0 (Sweep)

Game-by-Game Results (All 9 Innings):

- **Game 1 (September 28, 1932):** Yankees 12 – Cubs 6
- **Game 2 (September 29, 1932):** Yankees 5 – Cubs 2
- **Game 3 (October 1, 1932):** Yankees 7 – Cubs 5
- **Game 4 (October 2, 1932):** Yankees 13 – Cubs 6

Noteworthy Detail:

Game 3 featured Babe Ruth's legendary "called shot," during which he supposedly pointed to the outfield bleachers before hitting a home run to that exact spot, further cementing the Yankees' aura of dominance during this era.

Kentucky Derby (1931 and 1932)

The Kentucky Derby, a single one-and-a-quarter-mile race held annually at Churchill Downs, is among the most iconic horse races in the United States. Below are the outcomes from the 1931 and 1932 races:

1931 Kentucky Derby

- **Date:** May 16, 1931
- **Winner:** Twenty Grand
- **Jockey:** Charles Kurtsinger
- **Trainer:** James G. Rowe Jr.
- **Owner:** Greentree Stable (Helen Hay Whitney)
- **Distance:** 1¼ miles (10 furlongs)

- **Winning Time:** 2:01 4/5 (2:01.80)

Noteworthy Detail:

Twenty Grand's victory was considered dominant, with the horse finishing several lengths ahead of the field. The swift finishing time stood as one of the fastest Derby records of that era.

1932 Kentucky Derby

- **Date:** May 7, 1932
- **Winner:** Burgoo King
- **Jockey:** Eugene James
- **Trainer:** Herbert J. "Derby Dick" Thompson
- **Owner:** Edward R. Bradley
- **Distance:** 1¼ miles (10 furlongs)
- **Winning Time:** 2:05 1/5 (2:05.20)

Noteworthy Detail:

Burgoo King's triumph helped cement Edward R. Bradley's legacy as one of the most successful Derby owners of the early 20th century.

Other Notable Horse Races (1931-1932)

1931 Preakness Stakes

- **Date:** May 15, 1931 (Pimlico Race Course)
- **Distance:** 1 3/16 miles

Top Three Finishers:

1. Mate
2. Twenty Grand
3. Ladder

1931 Belmont Stakes

- **Date:** June 13, 1931 (Belmont Park)
- **Distance:** 1½ miles

Top Three Finishers:

1. Twenty Grand
2. Sun Meadow
3. Jamestown

Time Traveler's Note:

On March 20th, 1932, **Phar Lap,** *the legendary racehorse, achieved a historic victory at the* **Agua Caliente Handicap** *in Mexico, marking his only race outside of Australia. Tragically, just 16 days later, on April 5th, 1932, Phar Lap dies under mysterious circumstances in San Francisco, leaving his devoted strapper, Tommy Woodcock, heartbroken. This brief yet impactful period underscores both the triumph and heartbreak that defined Phar Lap's remarkable legacy.*

Will Patterson placed wagers on this race in book one of Retrorsum, he mentioned also, that the horse will die a few days later.

1932 Preakness Stakes

- **Date:** May 14, 1932 (Pimlico Race Course)
- **Distance:** 1 3/16 miles

Top Three Finishers:

1. Burgoo King
2. Tick On
3. Boatswain

1932 Belmont Stakes

- **Date:** June 4, 1932 (Belmont Park)
- **Distance:** 1½ miles

Top Three Finishers:

1. Faireno
2. Osculator
3. Flagpole

Notable Boxing Matches (1931–1932)

1931 Matches:

- **Max Schmeling vs. Young Stribling (July 3, 1931):** Schmeling retained his heavyweight title by knocking out Stribling in the 15th round.

- **Tony Canzoneri vs. Kid Chocolate (November 20, 1931):** Canzoneri scored a unanimous decision over Kid Chocolate at Madison Square Garden, solidifying his reputation as one of the greatest lightweight champions.

- **Mickey Walker vs. King Levinsky (December 18, 1931):** The rugged ex-middleweight champion Walker fought rising heavyweight contender Levinsky to a hard-fought draw, further cementing his reputation for battling larger opponents.

1932 Matches:

- **Jack Sharkey vs. Max Schmeling II (June 21, 1932):** Sharkey controversially won by split decision, capturing the heavyweight title in a result that remains heavily debated.

- **Tony Canzoneri vs. Jackie "Kid" Berg (April 18, 1932):** Canzoneri reclaimed the junior welterweight championship with a decisive third-round knockout.

- **Barney Ross vs. Battling Battalino (September 12, 1932):** Ross began his ascent to stardom, defeating Battalino and establishing himself as a serious multi-division contender.

Disclaimer

While every effort has been made to ensure the accuracy of the dates and details provided, inconsistencies may occur due to variations in historical records and reporting practices of the time. For a comprehensive understanding, consult primary sources, such as archived newspapers and contemporaneous records. These documents offer context, resolve discrepancies, and provide a more extensive catalogue of sporting events from 1931 and 1932.

Conclusions and Final Notes

The goal of this Time Traveler's Handbook is to serve as a practical and insightful guide for those venturing to the early 1930s—specifically to the fascinating region in and around Las Vegas during the years 1931–1932. It is designed to equip temporal visitors with the knowledge and tips necessary to navigate this unique period with both confidence and curiosity.

As with any travel guide—whether across space or time—it is impossible to predict every scenario, location, or interaction a traveler might encounter. However, this handbook offers a thoughtful overview, providing useful context, preparation for potential challenges, and highlights of the remarkable sights and experiences available during this complex era.

The early 1930s, though shaped by the hardships of the Great Depression, were also a time of resilience, innovation, and transformation. From the stark beauty of the Mojave Desert and the industrious energy surrounding the Boulder Dam project to the charm of small-town Las Vegas and the vibrant pulse of Southern California, this era offers much to explore and reflect upon. This guide aims not only to provide practical advice, but also to capture the culture, spirit, and human stories that defined this pivotal moment in history.

For temporal travelers, the chance to witness life in the 1930s firsthand is both a privilege and a responsibility. It's an opportunity to step into a world vastly different from our own—to experience its daily rhythms and challenges—and to gain a deeper appreciation for the endurance and character of those who lived through it.

May this handbook serve as a reliable companion on your journey—sparking curiosity, encouraging mindfulness, and inspiring a true sense of adventure as you explore the world of 1931–1932 Las Vegas.

Safe travels!

Due to the nature and intent of this guide, it is highly recommended that you store it in a discreet book sleeve or alternate cover to avoid arousing suspicion.

Acknowledgements:

• • • •

Enormous thanks to the ___UNLV Special Archives___ for the many tireless nights meticulously combing through the pages of the **Las Vegas Age**, spanning the years of 1931 to 1932. My goal was to bring back some of those forgotten businesses, restaurants, and nightclubs that once flourished in prohibition-era Las Vegas.

I am grateful for the wealth of knowledge I acquired from their remarkable collection.

UNLV University Libraries
Special Collections and Archives
LAS VEGAS AGE, VOL. XXVII, NO. 95 (1931-06-21) -
LAS VEGAS AGE, VOL. XXVIII, NO. 210 (1932-09-01)

[1] Image courtesy of *Las Vegas Age 1931/UNLV Special Archives*

[2] *Las Vegas Age 1931/UNLV Special Archives*

[3] *Las Vegas Age 1931/UNLV Special Archives*

[4] *Las Vegas Age 1931/ UNLV Special Archives*

[5] *UNLV Special Archives Early 1930s Highway Map*

[6] *UNLV Special Archives 1931 Las Vegas Age*

[7] *Las Vegas Age 1931/ UNLV Special Archives*

About the Author

Derrick Fitzgerald, the author of the new book titled "Retrorsum," has dedicated many years to extensive travels from the early 1980s to the present day. His journeys have taken him to every continent, except Antarctica. Alongside his passion for exploration, he indulges in various cultural activities, immersing himself in music and culinary delights from diverse corners of the world.

In addition to his appreciation for different cultures, Derrick has a profound interest in science fiction, particularly time travel, and non-fiction genres, especially technology and space travel. He also delves into subjects like Futurism and the profound influences artificial intelligence has on human civilization.